GIRL
IN THE
WALL

Titles in Dark Reads:

Blood Moon
Barbara Catchpole

Doctor Jekyll and Little Miss Hyde
Tony Lee

Red Handed
Ann Evans

Ringtone
Tommy Donbavand

Ship of the Dead
Alex Woolf

Straw Men
Ann Evans

The Black-Eyed Girl
Tim Collins

The Girl in the Wall
Tommy Donbavand

Badger Publishing Limited, Oldmedow Road, Hardwick Industrial Estate, King's Lynn PE30 4JJ
Telephone: 01438 791037

www.badgerlearning.co.uk

THE GIRL IN THE WALL

TOMMY DONBAVAND

"Go on," said my dad. "Go up and find your room. There's a new bed in there for you."

I stomped up the stairs, angry at my dad. Why did he have to get a new job in a new town?

It meant I had to move away from all my friends.

My new room was tiny! There was no way
I'd get all my stuff in here. I lay on my new
bed and sulked.

And that's when I first heard the crying.

CHAPTER 2
THE VOICE

"Oh great!" I said to myself. "I can hear some idiot crying next door…"

"I'm not an idiot!" snapped a girl's voice.

I sat up. "Who said that?"

"I did," replied the voice. "But I'm not next door…"

I looked out of the window. Whoever this girl was – she was right. My bedroom wasn't attached to the house next door.

"Then, where are you?" I asked.

"I'm… I'm inside the wall," came the reply.

I pressed my ear against the peeling wallpaper. "Inside?" I said. "Then, who are you?"

The girl began to cry again. "My name is Victoria, and I've been here alone for over a hundred years."

CHAPTER 3
THE SMILE

Victoria told me she had lived in this house a century before me. My room had been her room.

I pulled some of the wallpaper away and ran my fingers over the plaster beneath. "How did you get inside there?" I asked.

"I fell in love with one of our servants," Victoria replied. "My father found out, and he bricked me up in the wall as a punishment."

"Wow!" I said. "And I thought getting grounded for staying out late was bad!"

"You sound kind," said Victoria. "I wish I could see your face."

I lay on my bed and smiled for the first time in weeks.

CHAPTER 4
THE FRIEND

The next day, I came home angry again. "My new school is rubbish!" I said. "I'll never make any friends there!"

"You've got a friend here," said Victoria.

I found myself smiling again. She was right! I started to tear the tatty wallpaper off the wall.

I grabbed a knife from a box of kitchen stuff and started to scrape the plaster from the wall.

"What are you doing?" said Victoria.

"Do you still want to see my face?" I asked.

"Oh yes!" Victoria cried.

"Then, that's what I'm doing!"

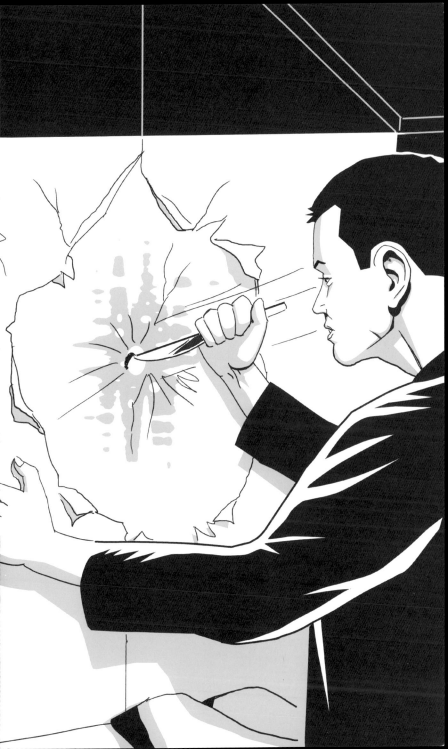

It took a few hours to get down to the bricks, then I began to dig away at the cement holding them in place.

"Hurry!" urged Victoria.

CHAPTER 5
THE TRUTH

I pulled the last few bricks away to reveal a human skull. It was a dull white colour, and very old.

"You are very handsome," said Victoria. "I'm sorry I do not look my best."

"That doesn't matter," I said. And I leaned in to kiss her.

The second my lips touched her skull I knew something was wrong. I felt cold, and I couldn't move.

I was inside the wall!

Victoria stretched, trying my body out for size. "Sorry I had to trick you," she said.

Her voice sounded like mine. "But you would never have agreed to switch places if I'd simply asked."

Then she started to brick up the wall in front of me. "I think I'll ask dad if I can move to another room…"

*

I've been inside the wall for over thirty years now. Victoria and my dad left ages ago, when he got another new job.

A new family moved in today, and a teenage girl has taken my old room.

She doesn't seem to like it much.

I wonder if she can hear me crying…

STORY FACTS

I've moved house a few times in my life, and I always wonder what my old home will be like with new people living there? Will my old room be filled with someone else's stuff? Will they put their bed in the same place? Will they redecorate the walls?

In this story, I imagined what you might find in a new home if not all the previous residents had left. At least, not completely...

Tommy
Donbavand

QUESTIONS

What was the name of the girl in the wall?
(page 12)

Why was she put there?
(page 14)

What was used to chip away at the wall?
(page 20)

What colour was the skull behind the wall?
(page 24)

How far forwards has the story skipped?
(page 28)

What made the author write this story?
(page 30)

Tommy Donbavand has written over 60 books for children. Most of them are so scary that you have to sleep with the lights on after reading them! His 13-book *Scream Street* series is being made for TV now. Recently, he wrote his first Doctor Who novel, *Shroud of Sorrow*. Tommy lives in Lancashire with his wife, two sons and more and more pets!

MEET THE ARTIST

John Charles is a freelance colourist and penciller who has worked for Panini UK on their *Marvel Heroes* and *Spectacular Spider-Man* comics. John teaches comic book art on Staffordshire University's degree course: Cartoon and Comic Arts.